Herobrine - Death Of A Monster

CW00902216

Barry J McDonald

Chapter 1

"Are you sure about this?" the witch turned and faced Gifu. Reading the look on his face she got her answer.

"You know you want him dead as much as I do," Gifu replied. "After all, it was because of him that your sister got killed."

"I know, I know," the witch said, "and I do, but you don't think that this is a bit of an overkill."

"Nothings too much when I see the look on his face," Gifu said. "I want to see a look of fear in his eyes."

"And his friends?" the witch asked over her shoulder as she got back to working on the device again.

"Their loss. I'm not the only one who wants them all gone. How do you think I found you?" Gifu said. "BuckSeth's the last person I thought you'd be mixed up with."

"You say that as if we were friends," the witch paused and turned to face him. "We never were. I built the portal that send Herobrine into that mini-game. That was as far as our friendship went. Like you, he promised that he could get rid of Herobrine. But we know how that went, don't we?"

"That was as much his fault as yours," Gifu said.

"How so?" the witch asked.

"You didn't take into account that witch of his."

"Is it my fault that she was delusional? Now do you want me to do this, or not?" the witch asked. Seeing Gifu nod his head in approval she turned her back on him and carried on with her work. "Almost finished. But I have to warn you, I don't know how this will work. Best case it'll get rid of him once and for all."

"And worst case?"

"We won't be able to turn it off. Once that happens, we mightn't just kill him, it could be the end of all of us."

"That's a risk I'm willing to take," Gifu smiled.

"You really hate him that much?"

"Do you have to ask that question? It took me long

enough to track you down." "So how is BuckSeth?" "Dead," Gifu said.

"Really?" the witch said, turning from she was doing.

"Yeah. Now are you finished, or what?"

"Done," the witch nodded and pointed to the small device in front of her. Joining her at her crafting table, Gifu smiled, "You do good work, you know that? Pity though." "About what?" the witch asked and suddenly felt cold steel plunged in her side.

"That you won't know if it worked or not," Gifu said, pulling his sword free. Watching the quizzical look on the witches dying face, he thought she deserved a response after all her hard work. "We could have been great together but you know how it is, I can't have any loose ends."

Reaching for the small device, Gifu picked it up and looked it over. Grinning to himself, he knew how this one would finish what he'd created. He now held the ultimate destruction of Herobrine in his hand. Whatever happened, Herobrine's days were now numbered.

Chapter 2

"You'd think we'd have heard of him by now," Emman said, throwing his feet up on the table in front of him. Getting a glare from SparkleGirl he sheepishly took them down again. "?Sorry."

"Maybe he's given up," Yeri said.

"I doubt it," Clara said. "He's like a dog with a bone. Once he gets a taste for it, you'll never keep him from it."

"Thoughts, Herobrine?" SparkleGirl asked and got no response. "Herobrine, you still with us?"

"Sorry, I was in a world of my own. Yeah... I don't like it," Herobrine admitted. "Sitting around here, while he's out there plotting my downfall. And knowing there's nothing I can do to stop it."

"Still nothing, Clara?" Yeri asked.

"Not a sign of him," Clara replied, seeing everyone look her way. "I don't know if he's found a way to change his code or if he's finally gone. But I can't find him with the room."

"Too much of a coincidence," Herobrine added. "Whatever he's up to, he doesn't want us to know what he's doing."

"I miss those days," Emman said and got a confused look off SparkleGirl. "You know, when the bad guy had an army or you could see him coming at you. But this waiting around, knowing that an attack is coming and not knowing when or where. I don't know about you, but it's not doing my nerves any good."

"Agreed," SparkleGirl replied, "even more of a reason to be ready for him. Anyone for a bit of sparing? Herobrine?"

"Maybe later, I might pay the samurai a visit and see if they've heard anything," Herobrine said, getting to his feet.

"You want me to go with you?" Seeing him shake his head and hold up a hand, SparkleGirl smiled. "Alright, but if you hear anything, you come straight here and get us, you hear me?"

"Yeah, sure," Herobrine said, walking around the table. Pausing behind SparkleGirl's chair he kissed her on the top of her head. Then nodding to the others he teleported away.

"Still taking it hard?" Emman asked, looking from the empty space where Herobrine had stood to SparkleGirl.

"A bit hard not to notice," Yeri said. "You want me to keep an eye on him,
SparkleGirl?"

"Nah, leave him. I think he just wants a bit of time to himself," SparkleGirl said. "Can't blame him. I've told him that none of this is his fault, but you know him. Too much of a conscience for his own good." Not getting a reply from anyone and the room stuck on a sour note, she tried her best to cheer things up. "So Emman, fancy a bit of target practice? Think you can out shoot me with that crossbow of yours?"

"It's not me you should be challenging, it's her," Emman said, looking at Clara. "She looks all sweetness, but I've seen her at work on the practice range. Almost as aggressive as you."

"Well Clara, you up to it?" SparkleGirl asked. "Want to show these boys a thing or two?"

"Yeah, why not. I could do with a good challenge," Clara said.

"What's that meant to mean?" Emman asked, putting on a hurt face.

"I just thought that when you and Yeri had changed back, you would have improved your aim..." Clara started.

"...oh thanks very much," Emman announced.

"I know, I think he's a bit cross eyed to tell you the truth," SparkleGirl laughed and ducked her head as Emman threw an apple at her. "See Clara, he couldn't even hit me and that's from the far side of the table."

"See what I have to put with, Yeri?" Emman said. "And

that's from a friend."

"Come on, let's leave these two," SparkleGirl said and walked around the table. "We can always protect them if Herobrine doesn't come back in time."

Laughing at the expressions on both players faces she took hold of Clara's hand and teleported away.

*****

"Herobrine, a pleasant surprise. Anything up?" the samurai that stood in front of the player asked.

"Banjo not here?" Herobrine asked, looking past the player and scanning the faces behind him.

"Banjo? Oh no he's got other things to do. Baz is the name," the samurai said and held out a hand.

"Baz? Can't say I've heard of you," Herobrine said shaking his hand. "Wow, nasty scar."

"What this?" Baz said, holding up his hand, "lost a finger too." "Battle?"

"Nah, devil dog. Got a bit too playful and chewed it off."

"Ouch!"

"You can say that again," Baz smiled. "Anyway, onto more pleasant things. So what can I help you with? Any news on Gifu's whereabouts?"

"Funny, that's why I came here," Herobrine said and smiled. "Any word on the hunt for Grober?"

"Nothing as yet, but I'm keeping my ear to the ground. Last I heard we sent twenty samurai to join with Captain Tonga's hunt," Baz replied. "Seems Grober's got himself involved in a bigger mess than this Gifu fella..."

"...and the sword of Stonewell?"

"No sign of it. That's whether he still has it is. But you know how it is, we'll never give up looking for it. So are you looking to join them? You want me to..." "...I was thinking it over..." Herobrine started.

"...between me and you. I'd rather you stayed here. You know, have you close at hand. Because if I was Gifu, I'd want to sort you out first, no offense," Baz said holding up his hands.

"...None taken."

"From what I hear, they've enough on their plate. It's best if you stay out of it. The last thing they need is you coming along and taking this mess with you... just my thoughts," Baz apologized.

"Makes sense I suppose," Herobrine said, resting his hand on the hilt of his sword.

"Sorry I couldn't be of any help," Baz said.

"Guess I'll have to wait until he shows his face then," Herobrine replied getting ready to teleport away.

"Wait Herobrine."

"Yes?"

"You ever hear of a guy called BuckSeth?" Baz asked.

"Yeah, we had a run in a while back. Why, what's he up to now?" Herobrine asked.

"Nothing anymore. One of our patrols came upon him, he met a grisly death a few days ago," Baz said.

"Doesn't surprise me, he always mixed with the wrong crowd. So what happened to him?"

"Tortured and eaten alive by a small group of zombies."

"Nasty," Herobrine said, picturing the scene in his mind. Being able to control zombies and knowing their fierce hunger, Herobrine could well imagine how the scene played out.

"That wasn't all, it looks like the guy that was torturing him enjoyed his work. They found a load of health potion bottles lying around the place. Looked like whoever did it, attracted them to the spot with some weird device. Then he kept tossing health potions at him keeping him alive until he got what he wanted." "Gifu!" Herobrine announced.

"You think so?" Baz asked.

"Captain Tonga told us about that zombie device of his. He used them before to kill a few portal police a while back. It has to be him."

"And this BuckSeth guy, what do you think Gifu would want with him?"

"I don't know," Herobrine said, shaking his head in deep thought. "But whatever it was, Gifu's just made his first move."

"And that...?"

Not listening to anything more the player was saying, Herobrine teleported away wondering what secret BuckSeth knew that he didn't?

Chapter 3

Pulling her bow string back, SparkleGirl closed one eye and trained her arrow tip at the target at the other end of the shooting range. Slowing her breathing, she paused for a second until she felt she'd done enough. Looking at Clara's crossbow bolt sticking proudly from the bulls-eye she planned on putting her arrow right beside it. Fighting back a grin she knew that this shot would win her the competition. On the verge of letting her arrow go, she jumped as Emman screamed out her name. Cursing his bad timing, she watched as her arrow missed the target by a mile and vanished into a nearby bush.

"You just had to do it, didn't you?" SparkleGirl turned to face him and found Herobrine come running behind. Fearing the worst she loaded her bow and got ready for action. "What is it, is he here?" she asked, looking past them for any sign of activity. Seeing a large grin on Emman's face and knowing that Herobrine rarely ran from a fight, she felt her face flush with embarrassment and quickly put away her arrow and bow.

"Great shot!" Emman said looking to the bush and clapping his hands. "Has she been like this all day?" he asked Clara.

Still glaring at him, SparkleGirl snapped, "Alright big mouth, where's the fire?"

"Tell her Herobrine."

"Herobrine, what is it? Gifu?" she asked as the player came over to her.

"Yes..." Herobrine started.

"... did he tell you that BuckSeth's dead?" Emman interrupted.

"He might have, if you'd let him talk," SparkleGirl turned to him.

"He was eaten by zombies," Emman continued.

Ignoring the player she focused her full attention on

Herobrine. "Is that true?
Zombies?"

"Herobrine thinks it was Gifu..." Emman cut in.

"I don't know," Herobrine said, "It looks like it could be. They found one of those zombie attracting devices. The only person we know who uses them is Gifu. Plus BuckSeth was tortured..."

"Imagine that old Bucky's dead," Emman said.

"Well good riddance to him," SparkleGirl spat. Seeing Emman and Herobrine look at her she continued. "What? I know it's what both of you were thinking."

"Well yeah, but like that. I wasn't his greatest fan but eaten alive by zombies. The guy was keeping him alive while those things were chomping on him," Emman said and gave a shudder.

"Really?" Clara asked.

"You do remember that he killed Wolfie2?" SparkleGirl said. "If it wasn't Gifu, it would have been someone else. That guy was always living too close to the edge. It was only a matter of time before someone killed him."

"Any reason what Gifu would want with him, Herobrine?" Clara asked. "I never heard him mention the name before."

"I honestly don't know. BuckSeth had his finger in that many pies," Herobrine said. "Money?" Emman asked.

"I doubt it, not by the way he was killed. I'd bet it was information. BuckSeth knew something that Gifu wanted," Herobrine said.

"Where's Yeri?" SparkleGirl asked, looking around for the player.

"Don't worry he's fine. I asked him to watch the high wall in case Gifu turns up." Herobrine said. SparkleGirl gave him a look and he answered her before she could ask. "Yes, I did warn him not to go wandering off. I doubt he wants to get shot by Gifu again."

"Good," she answered.

"So this BuckSeth guy, that was the one that sent you in that mini game?" Clara asked.

"How did you know? Oh I forgot, the room," Emman said.

"Yeah, I was watching you all at that stage," Clara said.

Feeling a thought coming to her that was just out of reach, SparkleGirl put her hands to her head and started to pace over and back. Seeing Emman on the verge of saying something, she glared at him down and snapped "Don't say a word." Seeing that he had got the point, she continued until she stopped and smiled. "I think I know what it is!" "Which is what?" Herobrine asked.

"Yeah what's your deduction, Velma?" Emman smirked and got a punch in the arm from Clara. "Hey! What was that for?" "Shush," Clara added.

"Thanks Clara," SparkleGirl said, "and if I'm Velma, you're Scooby Doo, Emman.

Or maybe that should be, Scooby don't." "Funny," Emman said.

"Will you two quit it for a minute. What is it, SparkleGirl?" Herobrine asked.

"Alright before I was rudely interrupted. I was playing everything over in my head, all the dealings we had with BuckSeth. Other than his loose connection to Calihan and the reptilians, or the mini game, they've been few and far between. He's always been a pain in the butt and he did kill my dog, but he was never really a threat to us..." "... well, I never heard any of the reptilians speak of him?" Emman said.

SparkleGirl nodded, "Alright, if I was to bet anything I think it's got something to do with that mini-game..."

"... you think Gifu's building one?" Herobrine asked.

"Hard to say, but it's the biggest threat we ever faced,"

SparkleGirl said.

"Or what about...? Nah forget it," Emman said.

"What is it Scooby?" SparkleGirl asked and saw Herobrine give her a look. "Well, he did call me Velma."

"Go on Emman," Herobrine said.

"Well I was thinking, anyone could build a mini game, right? Like, I could go down to the beach today and make a kick ass one. Heck, any of us could. If I'd enough time, I could make the most twisted game..."

"... so what are you saying?" SparkleGirl asked.

"What was the one thing that we had the most problem with?" Emman asked.

"Getting out," Herobrine muttered.

"Yeah, getting out. Only the witch turned up, we'd still be in there," Emman said. "If LucyPop hadn't got out first it would have been one of us. But only one of us would have got out. And even if Herobrine had the chance of freedom, BuckSeth would have

been pretty sure that he would have traded places with you SparkleGirl." SparkleGirl looked to Herobrine to see what he thought.

"He's right, either you or Emman would have gotten my place," Herobrine nodded.

"I don't know if I'm right, but I think Gifu's trying to find some way to get you out of the game, Herobrine," Emman finished.

"But wait!" SparkleGirl said, shaking her head. "We know he hates Herobrine with a passion. Wouldn't he just want him dead?"

"Maybe. But what if he found a way to make it worse. What if he could banish him from the game, like send him off someplace and put him in limbo? Wouldn't that be worse? Knowing your friends were out there somewhere and you couldn't get back to them? Knowing that you're going to live in that place forever?" "Wow, that guy is a sick pup,"

SparkleGirl shook her head.

"Or maybe he's working on something really cute, like maybe making an ice cream machine," Emman said and watched as everyone looked at him. "What? Just thought I'd lighten the mood a little. Plus I'm hungry."

"For all that hard work I think you deserve a few Scooby snacks. What do you think, Herobrine?" SparkleGirl said and turned to the player. Saying nothing in reply he turned and walked to Clara. Saying a few words to her, he walked away looking like he had the weight of the world on his shoulders.

Chapter 4

"Yeri! Have you seen Herobrine, or Clara for that matter?" Emman asked, shaking him awake.

"What? No... not since yesterday, why?" Yeri asked, sitting up and rubbing the sleep from his eyes. "Why, what time is it?"

"Early. Gifu's just attacked a village on the mainland, well the samurai think it was Gifu," Emman said and left the room as quickly as he'd come in. Running through the house, Emman called out Herobrine's name with no reply. Knowing this wasn't like him, he left through the main entrance screaming the players name as he went. Eventually he spied the player in the distance coming from a nearby mine with Clara just behind him.

"HEROBRINE!"

Fearing that he'd have to run the distance between them, Herobrine suddenly appeared beside him holding Clara's hand.

"What is it?" Herobrine asked.

"Where were you two? I've been pulling the place apart looking for you both," Emman said.

"We were in the mine, why what's wrong?" Herobrine asked.

"It's Gifu, well the samurai think it was him. He's just attacked Moorfield, killed almost everyone..."

"Moorfield?" Herobrine interrupted.

"I know, right on our doorstep..."

"... when did it happen?"

"Last night I think, there's a samurai here, he broke the news," Emman said. "He's at the beac..."

Not allowed to finish off his sentence, he found the player take his and Clara's hand and teleport them away.

Reappearing at the beach, Emman wasn't surprised to see the others all standing around the samurai quizzing him. Running after Herobrine, he got there in time to hear

Herobrine's first question. "What happened?"

"Herobrine! Moorfield was attacked yesterday evening," the samurai started. "How what happened?"

"We're not sure, it might have been Gifu. The whole place was overrun with zombies. They came in from three sides, those that tried to escape ran into booby traps and got killed. Only a handful of people made it out alive, it was a blood bath," the samurai said.

"Cowardly scum!" SparkleGirl added. "I'd like to see him try that here. I'd show him a thing or two..."

"... but wait, you said you thought it was Gifu?" Clara asked. "It had to be him, right?"

"That's the thing, we searched the place for those devices you talked about Gifu

using," the samurai nodded to Herobrine and then continued. "Nothing. There wasn't a sign of anything. It looked like they were all led there."

"But it had to be him, who else would do something as ghastly as that?" Clara added.

"We thought that too, until we heard some of the reports from the survivors," the samurai paused before continuing, "the players reported seeing Herobrine at the front of the group."

"What?" SparkleGirl exclaimed only a moment before Clara and Emman copied her.

"You know that's not true," Yeri piped in.

"I'm just going on what the villagers said. They said that a moment before the zombies invaded the place Herobrine was seen on the main street before vanishing," the young samurai added. "That's why I'm here, Herobrine. Where were you yesterday evening?"

"Now you hold on a minute, what your name?" SparkleGirl asked.

"Bombshell45," the samurai answered.

"Bombshell by name, bombshell by nature," Emman

mumbled. "Listen MR. Bombshell, you and whoever is in charge of you lot..." "Baz," the samurai answered.

"Baz?" SparkleGirl repeated the name. "Never heard of him. But you and this, Baz, can get that daft idea out of your heads," SparkleGirl said, putting her hand on her sword hilt. "I know for a fact that this had nothing to do with Herobrine, why would it? You think he's gone back to his old ways?"

Seeing the samurai mirror SparkleGirl's movements, Herobrine stepped in between them and held them apart. Turning to SparkleGirl he asked her to step down. Once she'd moved back a step he stood in front of Bombshell.

"So why are you here Bombshell? To break the news, or to take me in?" Herobrine asked.

"To see if you'd come with me," Bombshell muttered.

"In your dreams," SparkleGirl called over Herobrine's shoulder.

"So if I don't come with you, it'll look like I'm guilty, won't it?" Herobrine said and watched the player nod his head. "You got the short straw, didn't you?" Herobrine watched the player nod once more. "And if anything happens to you while you're here..."

"It'll look like you're hiding something," Bombshell added.

"Well I guess, I've no choice then," Herobrine said.

"Have you lost your mind, Herobrine? They're blaming you for something you didn't do, and you're listening to them?" SparkleGirl roared. Pushing Herobrine aside she wagged her finger at Bombshell. "Here I was thinking that you lot had a brain in your head, boy was I wrong. If SanJab could see the idiots you've become... Gifu's well and truly pulled the wool over your eyes."

"I'll go with you, Bombshell. Just give me a moment," Herobrine said to the player.

Turning around he found all the others look at him.

"I'll go and clear this up," Herobrine said.

Seeing SparkleGirl begin to protest he tried his best to stop her. "I know, what you're going to say and you're right, but I've got to clear up this mess."

"But Herobrine after all you've done…"

"I know, Emman. But it looks like Gifu's built a good case against me…" Herobrine said.

"… so he runs around in a skin like yours and they all fall for it?" SparkleGirl said.

"Well you can forget going alone, I'm coming with you."

"No, you're staying here SparkleGirl. I'll sort this out. I'd rather you got everyone ready for battle. Gifu just came into our neighbourhood and attacked us, he might try it again. I want you all ready, just in case he tries something here…" Herobrine said

"But…"

"No buts SparkleGirl. Take care of our family. I'll be back soon," Herobrine smiled and gave her a kiss on the lips. "I'll be back as soon as this mix up is sorted out."

Leaving SparkleGirl, Herobrine walked over to Clara and took her aside. Walking her a short distance away he whispered in her ear. Knowing that all eyes were on them and knowing SparkleGirl would want to know what they talked about, he promised her to secrecy. Happy that she knew what she had to do, he walked over to Bombshell and took hold of his arm. Once done, both players disappeared.

Chapter 5

Reappearing in Moorfield, Herobrine at once saw the destruction he had supposedly caused. Looking like any other village in Minecraft this one was eerily quiet. Apart from the odd samurai patrol that passed by, the village had the look and feel of a ghost town.

Looking to Bombshell he could see the young samurai thinking the same thing.

"Quiet, isn't it?" Bombshell said.

"There must have been at least a hundred players living here, the last time I passed through."

"You come here often," Bombshell asked.

"Nah when you've got a reputation like I have it's best to give these types of places a miss. The last time, me and SparkleGirl came this way we had Emman do the shopping for provisions," Herobrine said and pointed to his face, "when you've got eyes like mine and SparkleGirl's, it's a bit easy to give your identity away."

"Sure yeah," Bombshell muttered looking at them. Looking like he was uncomfortable staring at the whiteness of his eyes, he quickly changed the subject. "Baz is in that building over there. I'll go ahead and tell him you're here."

"Bombshell?"

"Yes?"

"Before you go, can I ask you something?" Herobrine asked and waited until the player came back to him. "This Baz... apart from our meeting the other day I'd never heard of him. You know much about him?"

"Not really. He turned up here out of the blue and took over from Banjo. Came with written orders from high up... that's as much as I know," Bombshell asked. "Why?"

"Nah, doesn't matter," Herobrine said and waved off the comment. Watching the player stare at him in confusion he continued. "It's alright, don't mind me Bombshell, just go get him."

Leaving with a confused look still on his face, Herobrine watched the player until he'd disappeared around the corner of the local tavern.

Now left on his own and seeing a movement in the corner of his eyes, Herobrine found a pair of samurai on patrol. Looking like they were on the lookout for trouble, one samurai gave him a long and lingering look. Watching as the pair went by, he saw one nod to the other and mouth the word "murderer" in his direction. At first surprised by their reaction he let it pass. There would always be people who believed the worst things about him, no matter what he did. Knowing that his friends knew he wasn't to blame was all that mattered. The others he didn't care about. Wondering if he'd made the right decision to come to Moorfield, he heard his name called out. Turning around he found Baz and a company of ten other samurai come his way. Taking up positions around him, the other nine players fanned out with hands on their sword hilts.

"Thanks for coming," Baz said.

"I didn't have much choice," Herobrine said. "Although it looks like the jury's already made up their minds." Herobrine nodded to his armed guards. "You really think I'm to blame for this?"

"You tell me," Baz said, "care to tell me of your whereabouts last night?" "I was at home," Herobrine answered.

"I'd heard that, I'd also heard that no one could find you this morning," Baz asked.

"So where were you?"

"I can't say..."

"Can't or won't?"

"Both," Herobrine answered. "All I can say is this had nothing to do with me... can I take a look around, see what I've supposedly done?"

"Alright then," Baz replied. "You don't mind if they tag

along, do you?"

"If it makes you feel safer," Herobrine replied dryly. "But are you sure ten men is enough? Like I did kill a whole village last night." "I think you're a reasonable man," Baz smiled.

"Maybe. But you should keep them close by, you never know what urge might come over me," Herobrine said and looked around the group. Seeing a few of the younger samurai tense up, he joked, "Just kidding, what is it with you samurai and your lack of humour."

"You think this is funny Herobrine?" Baz asked.

"No. But blaming me for this is," Herobrine said and teleported free of the group. Now ahead of them he beckoned them to catch up with him. "Well what are we waiting for?"

Led through the village, Herobrine and his armed escorts walked to the outskirts of the village. Once there, Baz explained what had happened.

"This was where the first of the zombies came through," Baz pointed, "once the alarm was raised some of the villagers tried to take them on, but it was a losing battle. Growing in size they forced the players back the way they'd came. Those that tried to flee through that street," Baz pointed, "were met with another horde coming in from that direction and over there behind that stone mill..."

"And they just suddenly appeared, with no warning," Herobrine asked. "No threats, nothing." Baz shook his head. "Then what?"

"I'll show you," Baz said and lead the group back through the village. Now on the other side, Herobrine couldn't help but notice the huge blackened craters in the ground.

"This is where they died."

"So this is where the booby traps sat waiting for them," Herobrine said and watched

Baz nod his head. "Pressure plates?"

"We found pieces of pressure plates over there in the distance," Baz said. "Sick if you ask me, letting those players think they'd escaped and then killing them all like that. Once the first explosive went off it started a chain reaction."
"And how many survived?" Herobrine asked.

"Five. Out of a hundred players, five are all that's left," Baz cursed.

"You think I'd stoop that low, Baz?" Herobrine asked. "I had no dealings with this

place. Why would I want to kill these people?"

"That's something I've been wondering myself," Baz asked. "What would Herobrine want with this place? Then we found it." "Found what," Herobrine asked.

"One of our patrols found it earlier," Baz said.

"We found your underground lair, or should I say, the locals found it and that's why you killed them all," Baz said. "Seize him!"

Confused at what Baz had said, Herobrine heard the noise of smashing glass a second before feeling something wet splash against his legs. Turning around and looking to the ground, he found the remains of a broken potion bottle at his feet.

"It's essence of soul sand Herobrine, so don't think of teleporting away," Baz called out from behind him.

Ignoring the comment and seeing the surrounding samurai quickly close ranks, he tried his ability and found it gone. Finding his movements slow and plodding he reached for his sword but never got that far. Hit hard on the back of the head, he fell forward and hit the ground. Then everything went black.

Chapter 6

"Bombshell?"

"Yes, Baz," Bombshell replied running over from what he'd been doing.

"Now that we've got Herobrine safely under lock and key, I think you should go get the others..."

"But..."

"... I know that thought of bringing news like this to SparkleGirl seems a bit daunting. But she won't be able to argue the facts when she sees them for herself."

"I know. But..."

"Listen, Bombshell. I've heard what she's like, she'll probably threaten you with everything under the sun but she won't harm you. And even if she does it'll make her just as guilty as Herobrine. Just give her the news and leave the rest up to me," Baz said. "And if makes you feel any better you can take two more samurai with you as an escort."

"If you're sure..."

"I am sure and that's an order, Bombshell. Now go do your job," Baz ordered and stormed off.

"Yes Baz," Bombshell snapped back.

Left on his own and worrying of what lay ahead, Bombshell picked the two largest samurai he could find. He didn't think it would make much of a difference. Not when they'd found themselves face to face with an angry SparkleGirl.

****

"They've done what?" SparkleGirl roared, on hearing the news from Yeri.

"They've only just come ashore, that Bombshell guy and two others... they said that they had evidenc..." Yeri never had a chance to say anything more.

Reappearing on the beach, SparkleGirl scanned the area and found the three samurai at their boats. Looking at them through a haze of anger she charged down the sand toward. Hearing her come toward them, she wasn't surprised to see the three pull their swords. She was looking forward to making them suffer for what they'd done to Herobrine.

"SparkleGirl wait! I know what you're thinking..." Bombshell pleaded and took a defensive position. Holding his sword out to keep her at a distance, he used his free hand to try to calm her. "This has nothing to do with me. When I got back Baz had some hard evidence to back up his claim..."

"Keep lying Bombshell, it'll be your last words."

"You want me to do something, Bombshell?"

Hearing this SparkleGirl looked to one of the samurai who'd step forward.

"I don't know who you are lady, but no one speaks to a samurai like that," the large samurai spoke, closing the space between them. "Bombshell might be afraid of you but I'm not."

"Glencar, stand down. We only had to bring the news that's all," Bombshell called.

"So you're the girlfriend of that murderer," Glencar sneered to SparkleGirl. "I saw him earlier on, the murderer. Told him that in fact. Wouldn't have gotten away with it if I was there."

"You think that?" SparkleGirl asked.

"Yeah I do. Should have been put down a long time ago if you ask me..." Glencar said and looked at the sword now sticking out of his chest.

Pushing it in deeper, SparkleGirl put her face up against his. "Nobody was asking you."

Pulling her sword free, she stood back and let the player fall at her feet.

"Anyone else got something to say?"

"Listen SparkleGirl, we're not here to cause trouble.

Are we Overflow?" Bombshell asked and watched as the samurai beside him shook his head. "Whatever that idiot might have said, that's not how the majority of us think. But we have to follow up on evidence even if it's Herobrine."

"You know he didn't do it," SparkleGirl said putting her sword away.

"Listen, all I was told was to get word to you," Bombshell said putting his own sword away. "Baz said to come get you..."

"Are you alright, SparkleGirl?"

Turning around SparkleGirl found Emman and Clara with their bows trained on the two samurai, Yeri was further up with what looked like a block of TNT in his hand.

"Listen Emman, Clara, we don't mean any harm," Bombshell assured them. "We're just here to tell you what's happened."

"They say he's done it," SparkleGirl called back over her shoulder, not taking her eyes on the samurai.

"But that's ridiculous," Emman added, coming over to stand by her.

"We found a cave under Moorfield, Baz says that it had evidence that proved that

Herobrine was there last night," Bombshell said. "That's all I know."

Saying not in reply, SparkleGirl left the samurai and joined up with the other three players.

"How do you want to play this, SparkleGirl?" Emman asked. "We could kill these two and go get him."

"Believe me a moment ago I'd have said yes, but now I don't know. I've already kill one, which can be overlooked. But if we kill them all, it'll look like we've got something to hide. It pains me to say this, but I think we've got to go along with this. Are you packing?"

"Packing? You're lucky I'm not sinking," Emman smiled. "I swear I'm carrying so much TNT, I'm afraid to sneeze."

"And you Clara?" SparkleGirl asked.

"Same as him, although more weapons that he has," Clara smiled. "Plus we've got

the armoury in the room."

"Me too, locked and loaded," Yeri added.

"Alright then," SparkleGirl smiled. "We'll play along for now. But if this goes bad, you all know what to do. Clara, you and Emman take the room, you're coming with me

Yeri."

Breaking from their little huddle, SparkleGirl waited until Clara and Emman had left the beach.

"Alright, Bombshell. We'll play along with this farce for another while," SparkleGirl said to the player. Leaving it at that, she took Yeri's hand and teleported away.

Chapter 7

Reappearing at Moorfield, SparkleGirl stood and took in the scene. Expecting them to be surrounded by samurai on their appearance, she found no one there.

"Is it just me, or shouldn't there be samurai here?" Yeri asked.

"Same thought as I had," SparkleGirl said and pulled her sword.

"You don't think they've upped and left do you?"

"Wouldn't make sense seeing as they wanted us to come here," SparkleGirl replied, still keeping her eyes peeled for any sign of movement. Seeing a movement she felt her pulse jump until she realized it was Emman and Clara. Looking like they'd stepped out of nowhere the two players jogged over to meet her.

"Wasn't expecting this," Emman said putting away his sword. "We took a moment or two to check out the place before we dropped in. It's a ghost town alright."

"We did find something, but you've probably already sensed it," Clara added.

"There's a massive amount of hostile mobs underground. All hanging around one area."

"Herobrine?" Yeri asked SparkleGirl and got no response. Looking to the player, he found her looking to the ground below her feet with eyes closed.

"I knew there was something there," SparkleGirl muttered opening her eyes and turning to Yeri. "As for what you said Yeri, this wasn't Herobrine. Believe me, Herobrine couldn't have got so many here in such a short time." "So it's Gifu then. It has to be him," Emman said.

"But why? I don't understand," Yeri said, "I thought it was Herobrine he wanted.

You think he's trying to take him off the samurai?"
"Could be," SparkleGirl added.

"But why attack Moorfield and then come back and

attack the samurai, it doesn't make sense," Clara said. "Gifu's the kind of player who likes to come in, make a stink and then leave again. Why attack this place twice."

"Maybe it was a trap to lure Herobrine here," Yeri added. "Maybe he planted the evidence to make Herobrine look guilty. Then he waited until Herobrine turned up and attacked again?"

"Sounds plausible I suppose," Clara agreed. "And Herobrine was here on his own.

So it would be the best time to attack."

"Alright, Yeri you stay with Clara. Keep your eyes peeled for any sign of activity,"

SparkleGirl said, "Emman you're going underground with me." "I don't that's a good idea," Emman complained.

Not listening to the player, SparkleGirl grabbed hold of his arm and teleported away.

*****

Reappearing in the cave below, Emman saw the horde of hostile mobs in front of him and screamed.

"Are you out of your mind!" Emman roared and pulled his sword.

"My hero," SparkleGirl chuckled. "Nice scream by the way."

"You could have let me prepare myself," Emman complained and held tightly to his sword. "And as for that scream... it was a... a... I was clearing my lungs after the teleport. You know... difference in air pressure..."

".... something like, you pooped your pants," SparkleGirl laughed at his wide eyed look. "Come on, they're mine kind of people." Still smiling at his discomfort,

SparkleGirl cleared her mind and sent out a message, at once the hostile mobs in front of them parted and allowed the pair to walk through.

"You're not going to tell anyone are you?" Emman

asked, keeping his sword trained on a zombie who had his eye on him. Looking at the decaying teeth in its mouth he let out a shudder. "Don't know how you two work with these things, they stink to high heaven."

"Alright at the back, screamer?" SparkleGirl smiled.

"You're all heart," Emman muttered, "And you can keep your distance too." Swinging his sword Emman slapped a zombie in the face and apologized when its head fell off. "Sorry, didn't mean to swing that hard."

Looking back, SparkleGirl looked from Emman to the head that lay snapping on the ground. "If you're finished with snappy there, maybe we could get some work done." "Sorry, but he was pushing his luck," Emman said and kicked the head away.

"Is it just me or have you seen one samurai yet, or even heard a clash or swords," SparkleGirl asked, forcing her way through the throng.

"Been too busy looking at these ugly mugs to notice," Emman said, pushing another zombie away with the tip of his sword. "They won't attack after what I did to snappy, will they?"

"Not as long as you stay close to me," SparkleGirl said, "but if I teleported away…" "Don't you dare!" Emman cried.

"Sorry, couldn't help that. Just thought maybe you'd scream again."

"Hey you promised."

"Yes I did, didn't I?" SparkleGirl smiled, "but I didn't say I wouldn't tease you about it."

"Thanks, you're all heart," Emman grumbled and kept his eyes on a creeper who started following behind him.

"Emman?"

"What? I swear if this guy even flashes once I'll cut him in two," Emman mumbled. "Eyes to the front."

Grumbling at the thought of leaving his back open to attack, Emman reluctantly looked to where SparkleGirl was pointing to. Looking but not believing his eyes Emman stared at the piles of samurai bodies that lay in a heap in the center of the room. "What happened?" Emman asked.

"Doesn't make sense, does it? I mean why would they all come down here and then not respawn top side?" SparkleGirl added.

"It's Gifu, it's got to be him," Emman said, spinning around to cover his back once more. "You think he's down here?"

Hearing an explosion above their heads, both players looked to the ceiling of the cave. Thinking the same thought at the exact same moment, SparkleGirl grabbed hold of Emman's arm and teleported them away.

*****

"Yeri! Clara!" SparkleGirl called on reappearing in the village. Getting no response and seeing a plume of smoke rising from behind a nearby house, they both took off running in that direction.

"You think it's Gifu?" Emman asked, trying to keep up with SparkleGirl and cursing his lack of speed.

"We'll know soon enough, Emman. But if Clara's got her bow out, my moneys on her," SparkleGirl called back over her shoulder.

Rounding the corner, both players let out a sigh of relief as they found Yeri and Clara unharmed.

"You OK, Clara?" SparkleGirl asked on seeing them, "we heard an explosion and..."

"We thought that was you?" Clara replied. "We thought you were on the run with the samurai after you..."

"... that won't be happening any time soon, they're down there all right, but they're all dead," Emman added.

"Really? How many?" Yeri asked.

"We didn't get a chance to find out, but I'd say at least forty," SparkleGirl replied.

"So this explosion," Clara said, "if it wasn't you or us... It had to be..."

"HELP ME!"

Hearing the call, all players turned and found a solitary samurai stumbling their way. Looking like he'd been in battle he walked toward them and fell in a heap.

Running toward the player all four gathered around him and tried their best to make the player comfortable. Pulling a health potion from her inventory SparkleGirl put it to his lips and watched him drink it. Waiting until the player had recovered a little, she immediately quizzed him about what happened.

"I don't remember much," the samurai said sitting up. "All I remember was that we got the order to go underground and secure the cave. It all happened so fast..." "What happened?" Emman interrupted.

"We were surrounded on all sides, the wall just gave way..." the player said and paused to take a breath. "Then they came at us, all those mobs I've never saw so many mobs..."

"Gifu? Have you seen Gifu?" Clara asked.

"Or Herobrine, where's Herobrine?" SparkleGirl asked.

"I think he they went that way," the samurai pointed. "They went across the green over there."

"Thanks," Emman said. "Will you be OK?"

"Fine thanks," the samurai answered. "I'll be fine now that you're all here."

"Right," Emman replied, unsure how to answer that statement. Joining with the others and starting to make their way in the direction the samurai had pointed, they heard the player called after them.

"So Clara, not recognize an old friend?" the samurai called.

Hearing the call, all players stopped and turned.

"You... know me?" Clara replied, pointing to herself.

"I should do, we spent enough time together," the player said and reached into his inventory. Taking out a small device he proceeded to push a button on it and smile. "Pity you'll die here with the others."

Realizing who they were looking at, SparkleGirl was the first to react. Covering the distance between them as fast as she could she slammed into an invisible wall and fell over. Looking from the spot where SparkleGirl had hit, the players turned and watched as the wall spread quickly around them. Closing them in in a circle, they all looked upward and watched as it closed to form a perfect dome. Over the shock of what he'd seen, Emman ran to SparkleGirl. Throwing himself on the ground he held her head in his hands.

"SparkleGirl? Speak to me SparkleGirl?"

Hearing her moan and rub her forehead, he let out a sigh of relief. "Thank God, I thought he'd killed you?"

Helping SparkleGirl get to her feet, Emman took a health potion from his inventory and handed it to her.

"Thanks Emman... what happened?"

"We're trapped SparkleGirl," Emman said and waved his arm at the shimmering dome that surrounded them. "We walked right into it."

Turning back to the samurai, both players looked at the grinning face on the other side. Watching his mouth move but unable to hear him, they watched him give them all a farewell wave and run off.

"How could we have been so stupid?" Emman groaned watching the player leave.

"And we gave him a health potion? I can't we did that."

"You're not the only one."

Turning around, Emman found Clara standing beside him. "I should have known he was here, I should have seen through that disguise."

"Not your fault Clara, we all fell for it," SparkleGirl

said looking in the direction Gifu had gone. "I just hope Herobrine's OK."

*****

"Wakey, wakey sleeping beauty."

Opening his eyes, Herobrine tried to focus in on the face that looked back at him.

Looking back he saw Baz smiling.

"Had a good sleep? You're just in time, we've had some friends call over while you

were asleep. They'll be so glad to see you," Baz said. Pulling his sword the player chopped through Herobrine's restraint and stood back. Holding a small device in his hand, he waved it, "Make any sudden moves and your friends are dead."

Chapter 8

"You don't look surprised, Herobrine?" Gifu said as he marched Herobrine toward the dome.

"I had my suspicions, you growing an extra finger gave it away," Herobrine replied.

"Just wished I'd acted sooner."

Gifu smirked, "Aw well, you can't have it all your own way. You don't mind me saying it but for someone whose back's to the wall, you don't come across that way."

Herobrine turned his attention from Gifu's smugness to the dome the contained his friends.

"Ingenious isn't it," Gifu said looking at it. "All that you care about locked up right in front of you, and yet just out of reach. I had planned on adding you to the mix, but changed my mind at the last minute. I was wondering, what would hurt Herobrine more, dying for his friends or watching them die? Plus if you died, who would have to hate anymore."

Ignoring the comment he continued staring at the faces that looked back at him and felt his anger reach boiling point. Pushing it down deep inside of him, Herobrine swore to himself that wouldn't let Gifu know that he'd beaten him. Waiting a second until he got hold of his composure he turned back to the player.

"You must really hate me?"

"Hates a strong word, Herobrine. But not strong enough for how I feel about you," Gifu said.

"You know I was different back then..." Herobrine said.

"... Oh I'm loving this. Is this the point where you tell me the story that you couldn't control what you did? Then what do I say? Oh yeah, that's OK Herobrine, I know you weren't to blame. Then we shake hands or maybe hug it out, then we all go our merry way," Gifu chuckled and then his voice changed to a cold tone. "That's never going to happen.

You took someone very close to me and you're about to suffer the same fate."

"And the people of this village? You think your loss is any greater than theirs? You think you losing someone is worth far more than what you've put them through. And what about the others, the portal police that you killed...?"

"All steps along the way to this moment..."

"You know you're kidding yourself?"

"How so?" Gifu asked toying with the remote control in his hand.

"You play the grieving player, but you're no more in grief than that rock over there. You're twisted inside. I'd say from the moment you came into this game. Let me guess you were a loner, a weirdo, everyone knew that there was something wrong with you..."

"Keep it up Herobrine and I'll push the button," Gifu said holding his hand over the device.

"You just needed an excuse to let that evilness out, and you used me as that excuse," Herobrine said and stepped closer to him. "Now anything evil you did after that point you could use me as the cause of it. Poor Gifu..."

"I'm warning you Herobrine, you say another word or take one more step and I'll do
it."

"You might call me a monster, but you're a bigger one Gifu. I might have been a monster once, but I've spent the rest of my time here making up for that mistake." "That's a joke and you know it," Gifu chuckled.

"Really, how many friends have you got here?" Herobrine said looking around him.

"Let me count them... oh that's right you've none."

"You'd be surprised," Gifu answered. "I've got thousands."

"Now you've really lost your mind."

"Really? You didn't wonder where all the samurai have

got to? Right now they're in that cave of yours. All there and all dead..."

"You murderer," Herobrine spat and took a step forward.

"Ah, ah, ah! My finger's getting very tired hovering over this button and we wouldn't want it hitting it accidentally, would we? And besides, it wasn't me that killed them, it was you. Well, I've staged it to look that way. So even if you kill me now, it's going to look like you've gone back to your old ways. Once Bombshell comes back here and sees the evidence you'll be on the run forever. All that good work ruined. They'll hunt you down for the rest of your days... plus you won't have any of your friends to call on."

*****

"You hear what they're saying?" Emman asked, pressing the side of his face up against the dome. "I can just hear mumbling..."

"I don't need to know, but I've seen that face before," SparkleGirl said, "I'm not going to sit back and do nothing."

Pulling her sword free she slashed at the clear screen in front of her and watched as it bounced off it. Not giving up and ignoring the comments from the other players she kept attacking it until she fell exhausted to the ground.

"What is it, SparkleGirl?" Clara asked, kneeling beside her.

"I've seen that look on his face before..." SparkleGirl sobbed.

"I don't understand?" Clara said helping her back to her feet.

"The last time I saw that look on Herobrine's face was just before he got killed by a devil dog," SparkleGirl said. "It was a look of defeat. I saw it on his face again a moment ago when he was looking at us."

"Hey, he'll get us out... won't he?" Emman asked. "I

mean, he'll just teleport in here and save us, right?"

SparkleGirl shook her head. "I've tried to teleport out Emman, it doesn't work. If he does try, he'll be as stuck as we are."

"Seriously?" Emman moaned. "So we're stuck here?"

Watching Emman pull his sword, SparkleGirl shook her head. "It won't work, Emman. We're trapped in here for good. No offense, but if I couldn't make a mark on it I doubt you will."

"What do you think they're saying?" Yeri asked.

"Knowing Gifu, I'd say a lot of gloating," Clara said.

"So this is it. We're trapped in this fish bowl and no way out," Emman said and then grinned. "The ground... we can dig our way out!"

"Knock yourself out Emman, but I don't think he'd be that stupid," SparkleGirl said and watched him hit the ground at his feet. Hearing him scream out in frustration she got her answer. "Nice idea Emman, but I guess he has that covered too." "What about your cross bow Emman?" Yeri piped in.

"Hey, great idea Yeri," Emman grinned and pulled it from his inventory. Calling for a TNT bolt, Emman looked for a suitable place to shoot at. Spying a small black device partly hidden in the ground, he took aim and fired. At first seeing part of the dome flicker, he gripped his ears as the silence inside was rocked by the explosion. Waiting until the smoke had cleared and the noise died down, he groaned at the wall that still stood intact.

"IS IT JUST ME OR WAS THAT A BAD IDEA?" Emman roared. "I THINK I'VE GONE DEAF?" Looking at the surrounding faces he could see that they were all in the same situation as he was. "SORRY!"

"THANKS FOR TRYING EMMAN, BUT MAYBE THAT IDEA NEEDED A BIT MORE THINKING THROUGH," Clara roared in response. "YOU DEAF TOO, SPARKLEGIRL?"

Even though she heard Clara's question SparkleGirl said nothing in response. Looking at Herobrine and remembering what she'd seen earlier, she wondered if this was the end for all of them.

Chapter 9

"So Herobrine, think you can kill me and save your friends?" Gifu asked, waving his hand in the direction of the dome, "you have to admit it, there's no way out."

"You think you've gotten me beaten?"

"Well from where I'm standing it looks that way," Gifu smiled.

"So what's your great big plan then?"

"Really, we're going to do this? You want me to lay out all my evil plans while you take this time to think up a cunning plan to save the day. Are we really going to go through that?"

Herobrine said nothing, trying to lengthen the time he had.

"Alright here goes, I suppose I may as well tell you, seeing as you won't be around for long. Well, with you out of the way. It's off to find Grober and take back the sword of Stonewell, then once I have it and the gemstones…"

Hearing them mentioned, Herobrine smiled to himself.

"You don't think you'll hand them over? I think you will, especially if it's for your friend's lives."

"You thought it out well, I'll give you that?" Herobrine said. "But you forgot something."

"And that is?" Gifu replied.

"You see the lovely Clara over there?" Gifu nodded.

"She's got the gemstones on her. I knew you'd try something like this and I changed my mind on hiding them. You were wondering where I was the night I attacked Moorfield, well that's what I was doing. I was afraid you might get your hands on the room and go after them, so I decided that the best place to have them was at home. I didn't even tell the others in case they let the secret out. So your gemstones, they're in there too…"

Hearing Gifu scream with rage, Herobrine grinned and chuckled.

"You've got a problem Gifu, you push that button and not only are you killing everyone inside, you're also destroying the stones. I think that's checkmate."

"DAMN YOU HEROBRINE!"

*****

"Is it just me, or does Gifu look like someone just run over his cat?" Emman asked pressing his face up against the glass of the dome. "He looks livid."

"Probably because of these," Clara said and reached into her inventory.

"You've got the gemstones!" Yeri exclaimed as soon as she took them out, "but how,

I thought..."

"Herobrine didn't want me to tell you. He was afraid that one of you might let it slip and Gifu would find out..."

"I wouldn't have told," Emman interrupted.

"Easy saying that now," SparkleGirl said moving from her solitary position to join

with them again. "He was right, none of us could have been trusted with a secret like that. After what he did on BuckSeth, I'd imagine he would have gotten the truth out of any of us..."

"So that's why you two were whispering and leaving in secret," Emman said. "I was worried that you and big guy were cheat..."

"In your dreams, Emman. Do you honestly think I'd come between SparkleGirl and Herobrine? No offense SparkleGirl," Clara said. "Besides I've only got eyes for you, dummy!"

"Really?" Emman asked, his eyes lighting up.

"Yes dumbo," Clara said, throwing her eyes skyward.

"Told you he was as thick as a plank," SparkleGirl added.

"Hey there was no need for that," Emman said.

"If you couldn't have seen that, then you're thick, end of story," SparkleGirl said.

"Now that I've got that off my chest, there's something else I probably should tell you. It's been killing me to keep this a secret, especially from you SparkleGirl. Since you've been so good to me and all."

"What did he make you swear to," SparkleGirl asked, looking from Clara to Herobrine. "I knew there was something wrong, the way he's been acting lately." "I've been teaching him to use the room," Clara said.

"But he can't, it's only me and you that can," Emman interrupted. "And why the heck would he want to do it? I don't understand."

"Now it all fits into place. I should have seen it coming, the way he's been acting lately. Asking me if I would've always have loved him," SparkleGirl said not taking her eyes off Herobrine.

"It was only as a last resort," Clara promised. "In fact I don't even know if it'll work, but he came to me with this idea..."

"Am I the only one who's lost here?" Emman asked, scanning their faces. "What idea, what do you mean last resort?"

"There's only one reason he'd want to use the room, Emman," SparkleGirl said, not turning her head. "He's going to use it to go back in time."

"What! When did this all come about?" Emman complained.

Chapter 10

Two days earlier...

Now with time to himself and away from the others, Herobrine thought over what his friends had said. Gifu was never going to give up and let him live a life in peace. If it was only him, he could put up with it. But he'd the others to think about now. His "family" as SparkleGirl liked to call the group, would do anything for him and that was his greatest problem. Never thinking about themselves and their own safety Herobrine knew he couldn't stand by and see them suffer at the hands of Gifu. It was his fault that they were in this situation, so it was up to him to make things right. Going to a nearby stream, he bent down and scooped a handful of water out of it. Splashing it on his face to cool him, he looked at the water as it passed in front of him. Staring at the reflection that looked back at him he muttered to it.

"So what are you going to get out of this one?"

No matter where he went, his history always got there before him, he thought sadly. Picking up a nearby pebble, Herobrine threw it at the face and watched as the once clear reflection was broken up in a ring of ripples the spread outwards. Watching the circles grow wider, he realized his life was the same. Every day the ripples he created a long time ago were still going through Minecraft ahead of him.

"If only you could outrun your past," he said to the face that reformed below him.

Not expecting to have an answer to that question, he found a solution come to him in an instant. Oh course you idiot, he thought to himself. Getting to his feet, he thanked the face in the stream. Like his reflection, the answer to his problem had been staring right at him. Teleporting away with a grin on his face, Herobrine left to pay a visit on the only person he knew could help him.

*****

Reappearing back home, Herobrine was surprised to find SparkleGirl on her own.

"Back so quick?" SparkleGirl asked. "No news from the samurai?"

"What? Eh no. I didn't get that far, I was looking for... where is everyone?" Herobrine said, looking around him.

"What's the guilty look for?"

"What look?"

"You know what look. That look, like you've been caught doing something you shouldn't be doing," SparkleGirl added, looking like she was enjoying his discomfort.

"Fine, I was just thinking about you all, OK? I was just worried about you," Herobrine smiled, feeling his cheeks redden.

"Big bad Herobrine's worried about us?" SparkleGirl asked.

"Stop," Herobrine mumbled.

"Awe," SparkleGirl said and pinched his cheek. "You're worried about Gifu that much?"

"Just didn't want the others to know that," Herobrine added.

"Believe me that's a bit hard not to notice. Even Emman's spotted it and you know how thick he can be," SparkleGirl said.

Herobrine smiled. "So where is he, with Clara?"

"Yeah, they're both at the target range. I had to come back to pick up some extra arrows. He thinks he's helping her by giving her a few pointers," SparkleGirl said and threw her eyes skyward.

"You're too hard on him, you know that?" Herobrine replied.

"Are you sure you're alright," she asked, stroking his face with her hand. "You know we'll beat him, don't you?"

"Gifu, doesn't stand a chance," Herobrine said and threw his arms around her. "Not when I've got my best girl with me."

"And don't you ever forget that," she smiled and pointed her finger in his chest.

"You wonder if..." he started.

"Wonder if what?" she asked, gazing into his eyes.

"If you and I still would have become a couple even if I hadn't taken the serum?"

"What do you mean?"

"You know when we first met, back when ChuckBone got you to trick me into leaving my home..."

"Now that's a long time ago," SparkleGirl remarked. "Not my proudest moment, lying to you. Thanks for dredging that back up again."

Holding her head in his hands, he smiled, "You know deep down I think I always knew you were lying to me. I was just afraid to call you out on it." "Probably cause you fancied me?" SparkleGirl.

"Hey, I hardly knew you. Although you did know how to make an entrance," Herobrine chuckled.

"So why all this talk?" SparkleGirl asked.

"Oh nothing, just reminiscing," Herobrine said.

"Happens to all you guys in your old age," SparkleGirl said and mocked him in an elderly tone, "I remember in my day... before that darn fangled thing..."

"Hey, shut up. I'm not that old," Herobrine said and chuckled. "I love you."

"Love you too," SparkleGirl said. "And I'd still love you, with or without the serum."

"Thanks," Herobrine smiled and kissed her. "Now don't tell anyone I was here. I wouldn't want them worrying about me, you know?" SparkleGirl nodded her head.

"I better find Clara, there's something I want to ask her about," Herobrine said. Then giving her hand a tight squeeze he teleported away.

*****

"Aw come on!" Emman moaned and threw his arms in the air in frustration.

"Told you I could beat you," Clara replied.

Looking down the range Herobrine saw Clara's last arrow stuck right in the centre of the bull's eye. Which would have been good shot, what made it even better was that it had gone right through Emman's one.

"Stupid target," Emman called and gave the command for a TNT bolt. Picking the target again he fired and blew it to smithereens.

"Somebody's touchy," Herobrine remarked looking at the smouldering mess in the distance.

"Hi, Herobrine. Bad loser if you ask me. Hates it when the girls beat him..." Clara said.

"Do not..."

"... Do too,"

"Please, kids," Herobrine said and held up his hands for quiet. "Save the fight for Gifu." Seeing the pair fall silent, Herobrine continued. "Emman I need Clara for a few minutes. Is that OK?"

"Fine by me, maybe you can ask her what she did to my crossbow," Emman pouted.

"Crossed eyes more like..."

"... Cheater..."

"... I'm not..." "... Are too..."

Seeing that he wasn't going to get any quiet time anytime soon, Herobrine walked over, grabbed her hand, and teleported away.

*****

"Everything alright?" Clara asked as they reappeared on the beach.

"Sorry about that, I know what he's like. He could go on for hours like that,"

Herobrine shook his head. "I just wanted you alone for a while."

"Sorry," Clara said and put away her crossbow. "I just can't help winding him up sometimes."

"So the bow?"

"Just a little adjustment with the sight," Clara said and watched as Herobrine cocked an eyebrow in response. "He had it coming to him."

"Right," Herobrine said and paused. "Can I ask you something?"

"Yeah sure. Everything alright?"

"Can you keep a secret?"

"From who Emman?"

"No. From everyone."

"Weird, but OK."

"And this stays between me and you. No one else, not even SparkleGirl."

"That's sounds a little more serious... but OK."

"I've got a plan to get right of Gifu once and for all. But I'm going to need your help," Herobrine said.

Chapter 11

"I'm sorry but that's out of the question," Clara said after hearing what Herobrine's idea was. "And SparkleGirl doesn't know this?" Herobrine shook his head.

"Oh my God. She'll string me up. I've seen her lose temper but I'm sorry you're going to have to find another way," Clara said. "I'm sorry, but you've got to come up with something else."

"I've thought it through, Clara. It's the only way to stop him."

"That's if you don't get killed in the process."

"I've thought about that and I'm willing to take the risk," Herobrine assured her.

"Aw please, Herobrine. There has to be another way. What if I kill you? How do you think that's going to go down for me? Especially when I can't escape from here. I'm sorry but you'll need to come up with another idea," Clara folded her arms and looked out to sea.

"Look I know, it sounds crazy, still does to me. But it's the only things that's guaranteed to work," Herobrine said.

"But..."

"Look I've thought long and hard about this Clara, longer than I can remember. But lately it's been getting to me. Now with you and Yeri with us... it feels like I'm putting more friends in danger."

"But you know we don't think that, we'd do..."

"... anything? Put your life on the line for me? I can't let you do that Clara, any of you. Hanging around me is just painting a target on all your backs. I can't let you do that anymore," Herobrine said.

"I can't talk you out of this?" Clara asked.

"No. I've made up my mind. I don't like to beg but if I have to..."

"Alright. Even though I think you're out of your mind. But say it does work, how are you going to use the room?

You know it won't accept you?"

"That's where you come in," Herobrine smiled and pointed to a pair of nearby rocks.

"You might want to sit down for this bit."

"I can tell I'm not going to like this," Clara replied, trudging after him.

"Before you start, I can't believe I'm even considering this," Clara said, sitting down beside him. "Plus if it does work, I'm not getting the room back, am I?"

"Sorry, but maybe you and Emman will be able to track down a new one. Plus at least you'll know Gifu won't be able to get his hands on it," Herobrine smiled.

"OK," Clara said. "So how do you think you can get the room to accept you?"

"I've been thinking about that. That was until I remembered you and Emman saving Yeri..."

"Taking out the bad code," Clara added.

"Yes. But what if rather than taking out bad code, you could put someone else's code in instead."

"Are you saying what I think you're saying?"

"Yes, what I need is some code from either you or Emman. Well it'll have to be you.

I know Emman will go running to SparkleGirl about this." "Maybe I should too," Clara said.

"I hope you don't," Herobrine said and looked out to sea. "I know they'll try to stop me. But this is one fight I'll have to do on my own."

"Alright. God I can't believe I'm agreeing to this," Clara said jumping to her feet. "Look you stay here and I'll be back. Maybe the time on your own will make you reconsider what you're about to do."

"It won't," Herobrine smiled. "I'll be here waiting for you. And remember..."

"I know, I won't tell anyone," Clara called back over her shoulder as she walked off up the beach.

*****

Seeing Clara appear out of nowhere, and still.on her own, Herobrine let out a sigh of relief.

"You weren't followed?"

"How could they?" Clara replied, carrying the bag that Herobrine hoped would help him. "For all they know I could be anywhere right now."

"Suppose so," Herobrine smiled and watched her place the bag at his feet.

"You do realize that this is going to hurt," Clara said, opening it and reaching inside.

Taking out what looked almost like a syringe, she continued. "And not just you." "I'm sorry, about that," Herobrine said.

"Heck for all we know, this isn't even going to work," Clara added and gave it to him. Going back to her bag, she took out two small bottles and handed them over.

"This is to replace what you're about to take. I've never done this before, so I don't know how I'll react. If I pass out you'll have to open those potion bottles and give them to me. As for you, I don't know how your body will react to a foreign code going into it."

"You ready?" Clara asked and held out her leg.

Herobrine nodded and held the syringe just above her leg. Waiting until the right moment, he quickly stabbed her in the leg. Looking to see that she was OK and getting a weak smile, he pulled on the plunger and filled it. Once done, he pulled it free and looked at the liquid inside.

"Are you OK?" Herobrine asked.

"Just a little light headed," Clara remarked, holding a hand to her head. Giving her one of the small bottles, Herobrine watched her drink it down in a quick gulp.

"OK, now it's your turn," Clara nodded to the syringe.

Watching how well Clara had done without complaint,

Herobrine didn't think twice of sticking the syringe in his own leg. Pushing on the plunger, he watched as it emptied into his own body. At first feeling a little weird at the reaction, Herobrine groaned as the puncture wound grew in pain.

"You OK?" Clara asked.

"Just a little sore, let's see if it works," Herobrine said and bit his lip. Blocking out the pain, he took hold of Clara's hand and got to his feet. "Let's see if this works then," he remarked and hobbled to where the room was.

Now at the doorway, Herobrine said a silent prayer that his plan would work. Lifting a foot he placed it inside the open door and found it touch the floor inside.

"It's working," he grinned.

"Well go on in then, we won't know unless you go fully inside," Clara said.

Lifting his other leg and now in the room, Herobrine turned and took in his new surroundings. "Hell of a place, you've got here."

"And the leg?"

"Yeah, fine. The pains almost gone," Herobrine smiled and tapped his foot on the floor to demonstrate.

"Ready for the grand tour?" Clara asked coming inside and sweeping her arm around the room.

On the verge of nodding, Herobrine found himself picked up off his feet and fired backwards out the door.

Chapter 12

Flung out on the beach, Herobrine sat up and marvelled at the strength of the throw. Like a magnet meeting another at the wrong ends, he realized that the room had repelled him. Looking to the doorway, he saw Clara running toward him with a concerned look on her face.

"Are you alright?" she asked on reaching him.

"Me? Fine. Guess it didn't like me," Herobrine smiled and got back on his feet.

"Well, I guess that's that idea out the window," Clara remarked.

"But it worked, didn't it?" Herobrine said.

"Yeah for two seconds, until it realized you didn't belong there," Clara replied. "Glad in a way. I didn't like that idea in the first place."

"Guess, we'll have to up the dosage the next time," Herobrine said and dusted himself down.

"Next time, what next time?" Clara stared at him not believing what she'd just heard. "The next time," Herobrine said, "you know try and try again..."

"Until what, you kill yourself, or me more importantly. Remember that dosage only gave you two or three seconds," Clara said. "To do what you'd want to do, that would take... I don't know, ten, twenty doses. I don't know about you, but I don't think either of us would survive that."

"Ugh!" Herobrine moaned feeling a stabbing pain in his leg. Looking down he could see a yellow ooze coming out of his leg.

"Guess it's not just the room, we have to contend with," Clara said. "Your body's fighting off the new code too."

Looking at the angry mark and knowing that she was right, Herobrine swore silently to himself. He knew his plan was a long shot, but he only required a few seconds in the room. Once he got to where he was going, there'd be no coming back. He'd find a way to make it work if it killed him, hopefully he wouldn't do the same to Clara.

Going back to the spot where they'd sat earlier, Herobrine and Clara walked back and sat down. Looking at the open door of the room, Herobrine allowed his mind to go over the problem once more.

"How many seconds do you think it would take me to control the room?" Herobrine asked.

"Forget it Herobrine, as I said you're going to kill yourself trying," Clara said.

"There has to be a way, there always is," he muttered to himself.

"Honestly I don't think it's going to work."

"It has to."

"This means that much to you," Clara asked and saw him nod back. "Even though you'll be going on a one way trip." Herobrine nodded again, not breaking his gaze on the room. "And what about SparkleGirl and Emman?"

"They'll forgive me in time. If it goes right, I won't have to worry about that," Herobrine said.

"So this is the only way to defeat Gifu?" Clara asked seeing him lost in his thoughts.

"No. We could fight him and we'd probably win. But I've grown tired of all of this. Once he's dead, give it a week, a month, a year, someone else will come and take his place. Someone else who wants to kill 'The Great Herobrine'," Herobrine said, using his fingers to make quotation marks. "Maybe it's all I deserve..."

"You mustn't talk like that. Look at all the good you've done," Clara said, "all the people you've got to work together, all the friends you've made."

"Sometimes you come to the realization that you can't outrun your history,"

Herobrine said. "Sometimes that past is never far from the present." "So there's no talking you out of this," Clara asked.

Herobrine shook his head, "No. I've made up my mind. Gifu's just been the last straw."

"You know if you do succeed, I might die," Clara said and paused thinking on what'd she's said.

"I'd thought about that too. But maybe the new ripple I make might make a difference in your life too," Herobrine said. "Maybe you won't find yourself in the situation you were in. But if we go through every possible scenario, we could be talking about it until the end of time."

"Oh what the heck, I'll help you," Clara said.

"You're sure about this?" Herobrine asked.

"Look at it this way. Who else can say that Herobrine came to them for help?" "True," Herobrine smiled.

"Emman said I should do something useful with my life. Guess you can't get any better than this?" Clara said. "Plus I've seen what Gifu's capable of. Be nice to put one over on him."

"Alright," Herobrine jumped from his rock and rubbed his hands together. "So how are we going to do this?"

"Leave it with me, but I think I might have a solution," Clara said.

"Thank you, Clara," Herobrine said. "And..."

"... I know," Clara said and put her finger to the side of her nose, "I won't say anything."

"Thank you. I'm sorry to lump all of this on you," Herobrine apologized and gave her a hug.

"Hey, what are friends for. Now off you go, I need to work on our problem," Clara said and headed back to the room.

*****

One day earlier...

"What's this?" Herobrine asked looking at the jacket that Clara had given him.

"One of Gifu's little treasures," Clara replied. "He

heard about it a while back and
    hunted it down. Think he won it in a card game or
something?" "So what is it?"
    "Sorry," Clara said taking the jacket from his hands
and opening it. "You see these, the needle points?"
Herobrine nodded. "The guy that created the jacket, he made
it so he could survive any attack. You see those pouches?"
    "Yeah."
    "Well you simply fill the pouches with healing,
invincibility, invisibility, or whatever potion you're looking
for. Then rather than having to take one at a time, you can,"
Clara said and took out a small plunger device. "Simply
push on the button and the jacket gives you them all in one
go."
    "Through the needles?"
    "Yeah, they pierce your body and give you the works
all in one go."
    "Wow, and Gifu owned this?"
    "Yeah, it was in his collection of artefacts in the back
of the room. I think he wanted it but never saw the need for
it, you know with having the room and all?"
    "I'd say he wishes he had it now," Herobrine smiled,
looking the jacket over once more. "You think it'll work?"
    "I think so," Clara said, "you'll just need to add these."
    Looking from the jacket to Clara, Herobrine watched
as she opened her bag to show it full of bottles. "What's
that?"
    "What you'll need... I've been busy this past few days."
    "But how many are here?" Herobrine asked, snatching
the bag open and counting them over in his head.
    "You've enough there..."
    "But I don't understand, you said that it would take...
how did you?" Herobrine asked, trying to get his head
around everything.
    "Ever hear of time travel? I went back about two

months. That gave me enough time to fill them all. I thought you'd be looking for this as soon as possible." "I don't know what to say," Herobrine said, "but thank you Clara." "You're welcome," Clara replied.

"Sorry to be a pain, but I need your help with something else," Herobrine said and watched her wince. "No, no. It's not any more syringes or anything like that. I need you to collect some gemstones for me."

Chapter 13

"So Gifu how's that finger? Looks like it's just had a new lease of life," Herobrine smiled.

"You idiot," Gifu spat, "you stupid, stupid, idiot!"

"Come on admit it, you've been beaten, now switch it off," Herobrine said.

"It can't be," Gifu swore.

"What do you mean, it can't be?" Herobrine asked.

"Did you honestly think I'd put you and your friends into something you could get out of?"

"What did you do, Gifu?"

"Nothing's coming out of that dome."

Looking from the player to the dome, Herobrine could see his friends watching what was going on. Seeing them shout to him and not being able to hear them, he wondered if they knew how serious a predicament they were in.

"Nice try. Now how about you put that device down," Herobrine said turning back.

"And what have you kill me? I mightn't have an ace up my sleeve but I know this is the only thing that will stop you from killing me," Gifu said taking a step backwards and looking nervously behind him.

"Really, you think that? I think you've got me all wrong Gifu. After all I am a changed man, well I was, until you started this new scandal about Moorfield. What's the point now? Maybe I should slaughter you right now this minute," Herobrine said and stood to his full height. Putting his hand on his sword handle, he saw a glimmer of fear in Gifu's eyes.

"Alright, let's call a truce, maybe we can come to an agreement," Gifu demanded.

"Aw come on, what happened to that I'm going to ruin your life and watch you squirm," Herobrine said and pulled slowly on his sword, revealing the first piece of shining steel.

"You wouldn't dare," Gifu said and took a step back.

"After all I do have your friends here."

"You also have the gemstones there, and I'll never let them come back into this game," Herobrine said and pulled more on his sword.

"I swear, I'll do it," Gifu said and lowered his finger.

"You move that finger a fraction more and I'll take your hand off," Herobrine said and pulled his sword free. "Guess we'll see who blinks first."

Knowing that Gifu was on his own and with no traps to fall back on, Herobrine could see him for the coward that he was. Watching him cast an occasional glance to the room and the open door, Herobrine thought he'd use it to his advantage.

"You want it Gifu?" Herobrine nodded his chin in the room's direction. "Want what?"

"The room, you want it?"

"No why?"

"Well it's no good to me... so how about a trade? The device for the room. You better hurry, I'd say Bombshell should be back here any minute now. Once he sees you here, I think he'll put two and two together and see that you were the mastermind behind it all."

Seeing the player take a long look at the doorway, he could see that he'd made up his mind.

"You do know that you won't be able to get them out?"

"You say that, but there has to be a failsafe, in case something went wrong," Herobrine asked.

"That was the whole plan," Gifu admitted. "Make the ultimate trap that not even you could get out of."

"And them? Can't you do something to get them out?" Herobrine asked, trying to read the players body language. "And I can't get in?"

"Part of the trap's make up. It can't be worked on with magic... or your teleportation.

It's invincible," Gifu said taking a quick glance at the

room once more.

"There's always a way," Herobrine said, "always."

"You're welcome to try. Now how about you and I come to that deal you were talking about," Gifu said and nodded to the open door. "When I get over there I'll put the device on the ground and leave it there. How does that sound?"

"Sounds like a man who's more interested in his own skin than revenge," Herobrine said.

"Let's just say I've had a change of heart," Gifu said and started to run toward the room with the device in his hand.

Watching him go, Herobrine turned to the dome. Seeing SparkleGirl make a cut throat hand gesture and nod her head in Gifu's direction. Seeing Gifu only a short distance from the room's door, Herobrine teleported there. Reappearing in front of the player he watched with satisfaction as the player ran onto his sword and stood there with a look of shock on his face.

"Guess I'll have my revenge first," Herobrine said and grabbed the triggering device from Gifu's hand. Pulling his sword free he stood over the dying player, "I knew you weren't going to drop it. People like you never have a chance of heart."

Coughing up blood, Gifu grinned. "They're all going to die and you won't be able to stop it."

Crouching down beside the player, Herobrine smiled back. "You've lost on that front too Gifu. You're not the only one with the ability to use the room. I'm going to use it now to go back in time. You think you've won, I'm going to make sure you never even come into the game. Now that's what I call revenge."

Seeing the confused look on Gifu's face lead to one of realization, Herobrine smiled once more.

"Enjoy your last look of Minecraft," Herobrine said and watched the player pass away. Now with the player gone and wiping the smile off his face, he teleported back to the dome.

Standing in front of the dome, Herobrine tried everything he could think to break into it. Starting first with his best sword and working his way through everything in his inventory, he watched as it took everything he had and not take a scratch. Standing in front of it panting, he willed himself inside and found it wasn't working. Looking around for something else to use, he turned when he heard a "thunking" noise behind him. Standing on the other side of the glass, he watched SparkleGirl wave her sword in a gesture to make him stop.

"BUT I'VE GOT TO," he roared and watched as she shook her head. "PLEASE,

LET ME DO IT."

Watching her bend down, he watched as she scooped up some dirt. Rubbing it against the glass, SparkleGirl started to write in it with her finger.

"What's, closing?" Herobrine asked, looking around him. Throwing up his hands in confusion, he watched as she pointed to the ground. Unsure what he was looking at at first, Herobrine could see what she meant. Looking at the original mark the dome had made, Herobrine could see that the perimeter was getting smaller. Putting his hands to it, he could feel it move back away from him. The dome was shrinking.

Grabbing a handful of dirt, Herobrine smeared it to the outside and wrote in it. "What do you want me to do?"

Going from what he'd written, he looked to the two letters she wrote back.

"Go? Go where?"

Looking over his shoulder to where SparkleGirl was pointing, he found himself looking at the open door of the room. In that moment Herobrine knew that she knew what he'd been up to. Whatever had gone on while he and Gifu had had their little chat, the truth had come out. Clara had broken her silence.

"I thought I could do it, I can't, I can't do it," Herobrine said looking at his friends faces. "Clara I can't do it. I'm sorry. I thought I could, I can't!"

Like SparkleGirl, Clara smeared dirt on the dome and wrote in it. Going to her message, he found the same two letters. On the verge of arguing with her, he found Emman and Yeri do the same.

Pounding his hands against the glass and wishing he was inside with them, Herobrine moaned through the glass, "Please don't make me do it. I can't, I really can't." Feeling like his world was falling apart in front of him, he watched as they mouthed the word "go" over and over again. On the verge of protesting once more, Herobrine found the dome step back from him and get smaller in size.

"DAMN YOU GIFU!"

Throwing himself up against the dome, Herobrine sobbed for all he was worth. Gifu had got what he'd wanted, he taken all he loved from him. Lost in a world of grief, he heard the "thunking" noise once more. Opening his eyes, he stared at the love heart that was drawn on the glass in front of him. Looking from the heart to the smiling face, he watched as SparkleGirl mouthed the words "I love you" to him. Copying her and drawing a heart of his own, he placed his hand over the spot where her's was.

"I LOVE YOU, YOU HEAR ME!"

SparkleGirl nodded and started to write in the dirt once more.

"Save you? But I've tried, I can't."

Seeing the confusion on his face, he watched as she started to write once more.

"ChuckBone".

"Chuck..." Herobrine started and was interrupted by SparkleGirl nodding.

Putting his hand to the dome, Herobrine watched as

each player took turns in placing their hand opposite his. Smiling at Emman, he watched as the player rubbed out ChuckBone's name and wrote "MaxDan" in its place. Nodding in agreement, Herobrine promised that he would.

Looking over the faces once more and seeing the dome grow smaller, Herobrine blew SparkleGirl a kiss and walked away. Making his way toward the room, he wiped the tears from his eyes and fought the urge to look back. He knew if he did, he'd go back to them. Reaching the spot where the room was, Herobrine pulled his sword and reached inside with the tip. Unhooking the jacket that Clara had left for him, he took out and put it on. Taking a breath and hoping that lady luck was on his side, he pushed the plunger and grimaced at the pain that ran through his body. Buckling with the pain he knew there was only one thing that could help him now. Risking one last look at the dome, Herobrine turned and saw that it was gone. There was nothing for him here now. Filled with a volcano of anger and grief, he took hold of room's doorway and threw himself inside.

Chapter 14

Reaching his destination only a fraction of a second earlier, Herobrine felt the room reject him once more. Thrown clear, he found himself lying in the middle of a large prairie. Letting his body get over the shock of its heavy impact, he got up and was met by a searing pain in his ribs. Opening Clara's jacket open a little, he slid his hand inside and felt a wet patch. He knew that wasn't a good sign. Pulling his hand free, Herobrine saw the familiar yellow ooze on his fingertips. But this time it was different. Mixed with the yellow he saw clumps of black and red through it.

"That doesn't look, Clara," Herobrine muttered to himself.

Like she'd predicted his body was starting to break down inside. Mixed with too much of Clara's foreign code, his body was fighting against it and killing itself at the same time. Searching his inventory for the small vials that Clara had given him, Herobrine drank down two of them and waited for their effect to kick in. As she'd promised he felt the pain subside and his energy increase. He knew it would only be a temporary effect, what was going on inside him now couldn't be stopped. Putting that thought to the back of his mind, he closed the jacket and tried to forget it.

Now back on his feet, Herobrine stood and looked at the open doorway that stood in front of him. The room had served its purpose be it couldn't be allowed to fall into the wrongs hands. Taking the packages of TNT he had prepared for the job, Herobrine tossed them inside and teleported away. Appearing on a nearby hill side, he hoped he'd gone far enough. Neither he nor Clara knew how the room or even the game would react to it being destroyed. Fearing that its disappearance would rip through the very fabric of the game, he watched as it exploded outward before falling in on itself and disappearing. Happy knowing that it was destroyed for good, Herobrine teleported away to pay his first visit of the day.

*****

Standing outside Herobrine's home, Herobrine again marvelled at its structure. He thought that coming back to it after all this time, it would have looked amateurish, but surprisingly it still stood up. Picturing it as he'd last seen it, torn apart by griefers, he knew how this great home would end up. But that wouldn't happen again, he was here to make sure of that. Looking to the wall that had only been freshly fixed, Herobrine remembered the spider attack that had almost killed him. Lost in memories of that night's fight, a dog's growl brought him back to the present.

"It's OK, Wolfie." Herobrine heard from behind him. Knowing that there was no way to reduce the shock factor, he slowly turned around with his hands in the air. Looking at the younger version of SparkleGirl and his dog, he couldn't help but grin at them both.

"Can I help yo...?" SparkleGirl asked, her sword drawn.

"Hi SparkleGirl, Wolfie," Herobrine smiled. "It's been a long time." Tapping his hand to his leg, he watched as his dog looked at him and trotted over. Allowing it a quick smell, he got to his knees and threw his arms around it.

"I missed you, boy."

Burying his face in the dog's fur he found his eyes flood in tears. "Best dog I ever had. It's so good to see you alive. Still taking good care of him?"

"I don't know who you are mister, but you better get your hands off that dog," he heard SparkleGirl command. "I'm warning you if you hurt that dog, I swear..."

"I'd never hurt you boy," Herobrine said and held the dogs face in his hands. Getting his face washed in a furry of licking he tried his best to continue. "You know me, don't you boy?"

"Herobrine?"

"Guilty as charged," Herobrine smiled, turning to her.

"But your eyes, what happened to you? You've only left a few minutes ago to get...?"

"Still fell for that zombie flesh thing did he?"

"I'm so sorry, Herobrine. It was ChuckBone he said that I had to..."

"I know," Herobrine said getting up. "I know about all of that. I also know he's on his way to grief this place."

"But how?" SparkleGirl asked, her eyes searching the horizon behind her.

"Don't worry he won't be coming, I made sure of that," Herobrine said.

"I'm so sorry. How can you forgive me after all you've done for me? I'll go, I'll never come back, I'll..." SparkleGirl said in a panicked voice.

"You'll stay," Herobrine said and put his hand on her shoulder. "Right now, he needs you more than he knows. So does Wolfie."

"I don't get this, what's with all this, "he" business?" SparkleGirl asked.

"He's out there right now, desperately looking for a cure for you," Herobrine said nodding his chin to the hillside in the distance. "He promised himself, he'd do anything to make you better. Even pull the Nether apart for you... or that's how I remember it."

"You remember?" SparkleGirl started. Looking at her face, Herobrine could see her finally put the pieces of the puzzle together. Once done she put her hands to her head and start to walk over and back in full panic mode.

"You mean, you're from the... and your eyes are because of me. Oh God what have I done? What did you do? Oh God, oh God."

"It hasn't happened yet," Herobrine said and put his arm around her. "I'm here to make sure, it doesn't happen again."

"You can, you promise?" SparkleGirl asked, looking up to him with tears in her eyes.

"What can I do?"

"Just one thing, promise me you'll take good care of him."

"Of course, of course," SparkleGirl said wiping the tears from her eyes and face.

"And another thing," Herobrine said and cupped her face in his hands. "Don't ever tell him about this."

"Yeah, sure, of course," SparkleGirl said.

"I better go," Herobrine said and left her to hug Wolfie one last time. "See you boy." Happy that he'd done all he need, Herobrine teleported away without saying another word.

Chapter 15

Walking through the tunnel he'd passed through so very long ago, Herobrine now had a better chance to take in his surroundings. The last time he'd been this way his heart had been broken by the loss of SparkleGirl and Wolfie, but now he knew that would never happen. Seeing a pair of zombies look at him in confusion, he couldn't help but nod and smile. His life had come a long way from that day. Finally coming to the lava fall that hid the witch's cave from view, he paused before calling out to her. Hearing nothing, he teleported inside and found her hard at work. Looking at her from behind, she looked a lot younger than he had remembered. But that wasn't surprising. Back then his mind had filled with grief and anger. Saying a quick hello, she found her turn on the spot and reach for a potion bottle.

"Is that the way to welcome an old friend?" Herobrine asked, with a grin.

"How did you... who are you?" she hissed.

Pulling back her arm, Herobrine teleported away just as the bottle left her hand. Now standing behind her, he tapped her on the shoulder and grinned as she jumped in fright. Looking past her shocked face, he saw what she'd been working on. Sitting in a goblet he found the mixture that changed his life.

"You might want to put a bit of sugar in it, it tastes disgusting," Herobrine said, picking it up and looking into the goblet. Holding it under his nose, he remembered back to the way it burned his throat as it went down.

"How did you do that...?"

"Teleporting? That was you and this stuff here," Herobrine said, raising the glass in a mock salute. "But you won't be needing it anymore."

Turning his hand over, Herobrine poured the mixture out to the witch's horror.

"Do you know how long that took to make?" she said,

staring at the puddle that disappeared into the cave floor.

"I'd imagine a long time, but as I said, you won't be needing it anymore." "I could kill you right now," she hissed.

"Yes, you could try. But I don't think you will. I can see that look of curiosity in your eyes," Herobrine said. "All those questions need answers and dead men don't talk. So what's it to be?" Seeing her remain silent he continued. "That player you've been haunting, that was me. Well the younger version of me. I know you've got some grand plan of making him into a monster and letting do your bidding, I'm here to say that that's not going to happen. We've both been down that road, and believe me in the long run, both of us regret it."

"But you don't understand…"

"… Players coming in here invading your world and taking what they want? I know all about it, and although I agree with some of your thinking, you're going about it the wrong way."

"I don't understand…"

"From where I've come from and what I've seen, you probably never will."

"But how come you're here?" she asked. Looking at the confused look on her face, Herobrine could see that some of the fight had been knocked out of her.

"Time travel."

"Me?" she asked pointing at herself.

"No. You'll be long dead by that stage. Let's just say you underestimate a player and…"

"Who?" she asked.

"I won't say, in case I can't get you to change your mind. But they're one of the best players in all of Minecraft. Even better than me," Herobrine said and smiled thinking of SparkleGirl.

"How can I trust that any of this is true?"

"You can't. But right now I could kill you and know

that all of this is never going to happen..."

"And you're not? Even after all I've done to you?" she asked.

"In the beginning I would have said yes, but now, no. Looking back I can see that you were only doing your best with what you had. Your potion was both a blessing and a curse for me. I caused a lot of pain to others because of it, but I also did a lot of good."

"And you want to undo all of that?"

"Let's just say it wasn't a fifty fifty split. A lot of people will suffer for what we do here. I think it's time that both of us stood back and let things run their course."

"So what can you tell me of the future?"

"I won't say, other than you need to be more careful with your handling of Chelka's gemstones. Some of you might think that hiding them is the best idea, it's not. All you witches were wiped out because of that mistake," Herobrine lied, hoping that this would spurn the young witch on to follow his advice. "You need to locate the sword of

Stonewell, it's the only thing that can destroy him once and for all."

"But why are you telling me this?"

"Because you deserve to know, and because he's one thing Minecraft can do without," Herobrine said and started to walk to the cave entrance.

"And what if I change my mind?" he heard her ask as he walked away.

"You could, but I wouldn't. I've warned Herobrine and others of your plan. If you want to make a difference to this world, help him. Work together. You'll make a bigger difference to this world than releasing a monster in it. I know you're not stupid, you'll make the wise choice." Stopping at the doorway he turned, "Plus if you don't, I can always come back here again. And believe me, you won't like it when I'm angry." Putting his hand on his sword hilt for effect, he could see that she got the point.

On the verge of walking away, he stopped and turned back. "You know what, it's only fair that you know the person that killed you..."

"... Who, who is it Herobrine?" the witch begged.

"Right now he's on the verge of griefing Herobrine's home. ChuckBone's his name.

You can stop him if you leave now."

"Thank you, Herobrine."

"Well if we're to work together, I suppose it's only right that we be straight with each other. If you sort out ChuckBone and get Herobrine safely back home, I know for a fact that you'll stop that time line from happening," Herobrine lied.

Watching the witch leave, Herobrine smiled to himself. There was only one piece of the puzzle he had to put into place, teleporting away, Herobrine went on the search for Emman.

Chapter 16

"Did you see that? What an idiot?" the player smirked and burst out laughing. "Have you ever, held a sword before?"

"I did, I did, must be just a greasy handle or something," Emman said bending down to pick up his sword. Feeling a foot on his behind, he found himself pushed forward and fell face first into the dirt.

"You see that MaxDan? He can't even stay on his feet," another player remarked.

Cursing them silently under his breath, Emman got to his knees and looked for his sword. On the verge of putting his hand on it, he watched as it was picked up and flung far away.

"Aw come on guys," Emman said, watching it land in a nearby bush. Getting on his feet and walking that way he heard a player call after him. "Give it up and go home baby."

"Way to go, Emman," Emman grumbled to himself. Why had he told them all he was a great swordsman? Now they all knew that he was nothing but another useless noob. Cursing his stupidity for telling a tall tale, he rummaged through the foliage looking for his sword.

"Emman?"

"Yeah, what? Something else you want to call me?" Emman called over his shoulder and got back to his search. "No really Emman, I think you're going to want to see this."

"What!" Emman spun and found a player unlike anyone he'd seen before standing in front of him.

"Is this yours?" Herobrine asked, holding out a sword. Once they made eye contact, Herobrine watched as the player back-pedalled as fast as he could and fell into the bush behind him. Looking at his friend sitting on his behind in a hedge, Herobrine couldn't help but chuckle at him.

"Who... who are you?" Emman asked.

"So this is what you were like," Herobrine smirked and

held out a hand. Seeing Emman think twice about holding it he continued. "Don't worry I don't bite. And if I was going to hurt you, I could have finished you off with your sword."

"Your eyes?"

"It's funny that, it's always the eyes," Herobrine shook his head. "All the things I can do, and most people are impressed with the eyes."

"Go on kill him!"

Looking back over his shoulder, Herobrine found one of Emman's group get to his feet and draw his sword.

"Is he any good," Herobrine mocked, turning to Emman. "You think I should run for it?"

"MaxDan, are you crazy? He's only the best player in all of Minecraft." "I take it you don't know many people here," Herobrine laughed.

"Honestly I'm only here a couple of days," Emman said looking like he was over his shock.

"Hey freak!"

Herobrine ignored the comment and carried on talking to Emman. "Boy you know how to pick friends, you were lucky SparkleGirl saved you from this lot."

"Hey freak I'm talking to you!"

"Who, SparkleGirl? You must have me mixed with someone else. You're saying a girl saved me? I'm sorry, but you're mistaken. You do know how skilled I am with a sword."

"Oh please, Emman. I know you too long, and you're always had trouble holding onto your sword. That and fibbing."

"I beg your pardon," Emman said, with a shocked look on his face.

"And forget that look I've seen it hundreds of times," Herobrine said casting his eyes skyward. "She was so right about you."

"You afraid to fight me, freeeeaaaak!"

Turning around Herobrine found MaxDan standing in front of him with his sword held for an attack.

"Yeah, crazy eyes I'm talking to you," MaxDan snarled.

"Now that's a new one, crazy eyes," Herobrine repeated. "In all the time I've been around, no one's ever called me that. Be careful with that sword, I wouldn't want to see you hurt yourself."

"Oh it won't be me, it'll be you," MaxDan said waving the tip of his sword in a teasing manner.

"Excuse me, Emman. We'll talk more in a minute, Gobby here wants to fight me," Herobrine said and cocked his head in the player's direction.

Hearing himself referred to Gobby, had the effect Herobrine thought it would.

Teleporting away he stood behind MaxDan and watched as the player sliced through thin air.

"What the?"

"Behind you MaxDan," Herobrine said and tapped the player on the shoulder. Giving him just enough time to turn his head, Herobrine drew back his arm and thumped the player full in the face. Watching him fall like a puppet whose strings had been cut, he stood over the unconscious player and smiled.

"That's for calling me a freak, and that's from SparkleGirl. Even though you haven't met her yet."

Finished with their little one sided conversation, Herobrine turned and found MaxDan's group thinking over what to do next.

"Guys, don't bother because I'll do the same to the next one who comes at me. Or maybe I'll lose my temper and draw this," Herobrine said and put his hand on his sword hilt. Seeing no one rise to the challenge, he turned to Emman once more. "Let's leave this bunch of losers."

"You'll pay for that, once MaxDan finds out who you are, I know he'll make you pay," a voice called out.

"Tell him I'll be waiting," Herobrine said and took Emman's hand. "Emman you're going to love this bit."

Not giving the player a chance to say anything more, he took hold of Emman's hand and teleported the two of them away.

Chapter 17

Reappearing from their teleportation, Emman pulled his hand free of Herobrine and ran a short distance away. Putting his hands on either side of his waist he doubled over and made a gagging noise.

"I'm going to be sick," Emman complained and put the back of his hand to his mouth.

"Guess, it's the same with you too," Herobrine smiled, seeing the look Emman gave him. "Oh I forgot to say, you've never liked teleporting."

"Thanks," Emman said and found a nearby stone to sit on.

"Well it's better than being back with that crowd," Herobrine winced. Pulling open his jacket and examining his wound, he could see that his sudden move punching MaxDan had made it a lot worse. "Bunch of bullies if you ask me?"

Seeing Emman look at his hand, he quickly cleaned it in his clothes.

"You OK? That looks like a nasty wound you've got?" Emman asked.

"I'll be fine, I've had worse," Herobrine replied and waved the comment away.

"OK... you promise that's the last time we do that teleporting thing?" Emman asked.

Herobrine nodded. "And you're not going to kill me?" Herobrine nodded once more. "So what do you want? You turn up out of the blue, knock out one of the toughest guys I know..."

"Believe me you've known tougher," Herobrine smiled.

"And that thing, that thing you're doing right now. As if you know me. I think I'd remember someone like you, those eyes..."

"Enough about the eyes, alright. What is it with you and my eyes?" Herobrine said.

"Where are we?" Emman asked eventually taking in his surroundings. "Have we travelled far?"

"Yeah, a little. If you think that four or five days on horseback are far," Herobrine said. Watching the player turn around he saw him catch sight of his home.

"Wow, what's that?" Emman asked and gave out a soft whistle.

"Good isn't it," Herobrine said.

"Yours?" Emman asked.

"Used to be, it's someone else's now. That's why I brought you here. I want you to meet him."

"Right. But I don't understand..."

"Don't be nervous, he's a good guy. I know you'll like him. The girl on the other hand may take a little while to get used to..."

"A girl? You should know all the ladies love me," Emman boasted and fixed his hair. "I'd go easy on that," Herobrine smiled. "I think she likes the silent brooding type." "Gotcha, so what am I doing here again?" Emman asked.

"I've asked Herobrine to teach you. He's one of the best you'll find around these parts. Plus I think he could do with someone like you around the place," Herobrine said.

"He'll probably say he doesn't, and that he likes living alone, don't believe it." "So why are you doing all this?" Emman asked.

"Let's just say, I was asked to find the three best players in all of Minecraft to team up. Your name came up as one of them..." "Me? You're kidding," Emman said.

"Do I look like the kidding type? Especially with these eyes," Herobrine asked, putting on his most serious face.

"Well I guess not, but me?" "Are you looking for adventures?" Emman nodded.

"Friends that would die for you?"

"Hey, who said anything about dying?" Emman

stuttered.

"OK maybe a bit too far," Herobrine muttered to himself. "OK friends that would do anything for you?"

Emman nodded.

"Well you'll find it all if you stick with those two," Herobrine said. "As for the girl, she'll probably tell you that she doesn't like you. But I know a good looking player like you will win her over."

"She'll be putty in my hands," Emman said and again fixed his hair. Seeing this and knowing SparkleGirl like he did, Herobrine held back a laugh. He could only imagine the fireworks that were going to go off when the two of them got together. Thinking on it, he pitied Herobrine caught in the middle of the two of them.

"They're expecting you," Herobrine said and pointed the way. "Go on go now and remember stick together no matter what. You'll be glad you did. Now off you go."

Watching the player trudge off in the direction of his home, Herobrine couldn't help but smile at what he saw. He knew by coming back he'd changed everything. There'd be no monster now running through Minecraft leaving destruction and death in its path. There also wouldn't be any other monsters like Gifu being made because of his actions. Knowing that he'd changed history forever, he also knew that new events and battles would come and replace them. Who knew what trouble this new Herobrine, SparkleGirl and Emman would find themselves in? Or maybe they'd just leave peaceful lives, building and tending to crops. Grinning to himself, he knew that wouldn't happen. Knowing the three of them like he did, he knew they've never be happy living a quiet life.

Seeing Emman finally reach his new home and Wolfie come running out to meet him, Herobrine sat down and made himself comfortable. It wasn't long before the other two players came out to see what the commotion was.

Pulling out the last potion bottle from his inventory he drank it down and watched the scene play out in front of him. He'd done what he set out to do. Feeling the pain from his mortal wound kick in again, he pulled back his jacket and saw that the damage had spread. It wouldn't be long now, he thought.

Staring at his old home, he pictured the scene inside and thought of happier times

with his own SparkleGirl and Emman. Then closing his eyes, he uttered the words the witch had said to him long, long ago. "Herobrine is dead, long live Herobrine."

Letting the wound take him, he vanished from sight.

THE END.

Thank You

As always I want to thank you for being a fan of these books. What started as a single book, Herobrine - Birth Of A Monster, quickly grew into a series because of great readers like you. Never in a million years did I ever think I could write a book (although some people might say that that's still true), to finishing this series after fourteen books is something that still boggles my mind. I hope you enjoyed this book and although sad, I hope it ended in a way that was pleasing for all of you. And for those of you that cried at parts of the story, don't be ashamed, I cried writing them. In some ways after writing about these characters for so long they've become as close as any family member. At this point I've don't know what else to say but to finish with another thank you. Who knows maybe we'll meet again in another book series.

Take care and God bless.

Barry.

Printed in Great Britain
by Amazon